CONTENTS

The Rebiking Centre

"Just look at that!" cried Steinasaurus Rex to his friend and creator Frank N. Stein. There in front of them was a huge sign.

"It looks great, Steinasaurus," said Frank, glowing with pride. "But you know it should be recycling not rebiking."

"I call it rebiking," insisted Steinasaurus. "Monsters prefer rebiking," and he began to munch his way through pile of bricks.

Frank sighed, "Don't eat the bricks, they're for building your centre."

"But they're nice, my boy Frank."

"That's not the point," replied Frank.

"Don't you think I've chosen a good way to spend all the money I've earned eating rubbish all over the world, my boy Frank?"

"It's very good, monster," smiled his friend. "They'll be bringing paper and glass here from all over the country."

But the monster was too busy munching away at a digger truck to hear.

"That's better," he grinned. "I felt peckish."

Then he picked up a piece of scaffolding and wolfed it down. Just as Steinasaurus was about to eat the cement mixer the foreman rushed up, mopping his brow.

"Steinasaurus Rex, will you put that thing down, put it down this very second. Honestly Frank, I know this monster you made eats rubbish, but how are we supposed to get this building finished if he eats all the material and the machines."

"Sorry," mumbled the monster, "I get hungry, you see."

"I'll keep him away," interrupted Frank. "I'll see to it that he doesn't come to the site again until the building is finished."

"But I want to watch my centre being built," grumbled the monster.

"Steinasaurus Rex, if you're here the building won't be finished on time. I tell you what. Let's go home and organise the best party ever to celebrate the opening of the biggest Recycling Centre in the whole wide world."

"A party!" yelled Steinasaurus. "I would love a party. Listen everyone, you're all invited to my party. Come on, Frank, let's go, we've got big plans to make."

So the big truck that transported Steinasaurus Rex around picked them up, and they went off waving to the workmen.

That evening Frank and his monster sat in the garden outside the monster's hut and made a list of who they were going to invite to the party. It came to nearly 300 people. Frank designed an invitation.

COME and help us to celebrate thE Opening oF the world's First and biggesT Rebiking Centre.
Frank. N. stein and steinasaurus Rex invite you To the opening of the steinasaurus Rex Rebiking Centre on saturday 15th June to be followeD by a wonderful ParTY at: Lot 107, The JuBilee IndustriaL Estate, South Brockton

RSVP steinasaurus Rex.

"We ought to get someone famous to open your centre," Frank told the monster.

"I don't know anyone famous," said the monster, shaking his head. "Do you?"

"Maybe one of the stars from a Frankenstein film?" suggested Frank.

"Oooh," said the monster, his eyes lighting up, "I'd love to see one of those films. Could you get one on video for me?"

So Frank and the monster went to the video shop, and Frank went in and got the movie *Frankenstein*. Back at the house Frank put it on and the monster sat in the garden with his head stuck through the French windows, tears running down his face.

"That poor monster, everyone was so mean to him that he turned into a bad monster. Not like me, eh Frank?"

"No you were always a nice monster," said Frank, holding the monster's hand and squeezing it.

"But I might have been bad, Frank. If everyone had run away and been scared."

"You were lucky," Frank told him. "You were made by children and we wouldn't be that daft."

"I like that pretty lady in the film," said the monster. "Do you thing she might come and open my Rebiking Centre?"

"We could ask her," nodded Frank. "I think I read somewhere that she was very interested in green issues."

"Does that mean she would approve of my Rebiking Centre?" asked the monster.

"Probably," said Frank. "We'll write her a letter together and explain the situation, and then maybe she'll agree to come."

"We'll do it as soon as the film is over," agreed the monster, and he continued to cry over the bad treatment of the monster until the film ended.

Brides of Frankenstein

"There's a letter for me," yelled the monster, as Frank opened the gate on his way home from school. "Quick, read it to me, it may be from the lady in the film."

"I thought you were learning to read," said Frank, as he took the letter.

"Oh I am, my boy Frank, but I find people's writing a bit difficult. Read it please, please, please!"

Frank opened the envelope and read:

Dear Steinasaurus Rex and Frank N. Stein,

Thank you so much for your kind invitation
to open your recycling centre (I presume the
rebiking was a joke or a mistake.) I am
delighted to accept. As you probably know,   I
am concerned about the environment and very
much approve of the new centre you are
planning.

Looking forward to meeting you on the
fifteenth of June.

Yours

Marina Dodgson.

"She's going to come!" shouted the
monster and he picked Frank up and threw
him in the air.

"Put me down," yelled Frank, kicking his legs in the air and shaking his fist at Steinasaurus Rex.

"Sorry," said the monster, "I got a bit carried away."

"No you didn't, it was me who got carried away," grumbled Frank, straightening out his clothes. "Now don't do that again Steinasaurus Rex, it makes me feel seasick."

As the day for the grand opening of the Rebiking Centre approached the monster and the Steins began to feel very excited.

On the fourteenth of June, the day before the party – they drove out to the centre.

"It hardly looks like the same place," said Mrs Stein. "Those bowls of flowers make

all the difference, and the tables with umbrellas give it a lovely atmosphere."

"Yes," agreed Mr Stein. "And all the bunting and the flags. It's very colourful."

"You're right," said Frank. "And when that big sheet thing comes down revealing the name, 'The Steinasaurus Rex Rebiking Centre,' it will look very grand."

The next day, people swarmed into the centre. They were all given drinks and then they waited for the official opening. On the dot of 3pm Marina Dodgson climbed on to the stage. Behind her sat the Steins, the monster, the mayor and the council. As she stood up to speak lots of flashes went off.

"It's only the newspaper people taking pictures," Frank whispered to the monster, who was looking a bit alarmed.

"Having appeared in the film of Frankenstein," she began, I was a bit nervous of meeting another Frank N. Stein and his monster, but they turned out to be quite different from the originals."

Everyone laughed. "And now I have great pleasure in declaring this Recycling Centre. . ."

"Rebiking," yelled the monster fiercely. "Rebiking Centre! What's the matter with everyone?"

"This. . . um. . . Rebiking Centre – open," said the actress. "I would like to use this occasion to remind everyone that the earth's resources are limited and it is crucial that we recycle as much as we can. I hope that this centre, kindly donated to the nation by Steinasaurus Rex, will be much used and will be only the first of its kind."

Everyone clapped and cheered. The actress pulled the cord and there, in bright red letters was: 'THE STEINASAURUS REX REBIKING CENTRE – bring your paper, glass and cans to be rebiked here'.

Steinasaurus took the microphone and ate it.

"Oh no," groaned Frank N. Stein "You were supposed to make a speech."

"I'll shout," said the monster. "I've got a big voice, I was just a bit peckish, my boy Frank, nothing to get het up about." The monster turned to address the crowd.

"Thank you all for coming to the opening of my Rebiking Centre. I hope you will all use it, particularly for paper. You see, I really like reading books and I'm very worried there might not be enough paper for all the books, so please help. There's food and drink and a band, so off you go everyone, and have a good time."

Everyone did have a good time. Marina Dodgson danced with Mr Stein, and then Frank, and then agreed to teach the monster how to dance. He really enjoyed himself. The monster party didn't end until one o'clock in the morning and all the parents were having so much fun they didn't even notice the time.

After the opening of the Rebiking Centre, the monster was rather quiet. Each day he went off and ate the rubbish as usual but everyone noticed that Steinasaurus Rex wasn't quite himself. He spent a lot of time alone staring into space and moping.

"He's not eating as much as he used to," the dustmen told Frank.

"He never comes to school to learn to read any more," complained the children.

"He doesn't talk to me as much as he used to either," commented Frank sadly. "I'll try to find out what the problem is."

So Frank knocked on the door of the monster's hut and called out.

"Hello, are you home? Can I come in?"

"If you want to," came the listless reply.

"What's up?" asked Frank.

"I'm in love," replied the monster, "with Marina Dodgson."

"But she's a human," said Frank. "She's very famous and beautiful."

"I know," said the monster, tears running down his cheeks. "But there are no monsters for me to love, my boy Frank. I'll have to be lonely for ever."

"Oh dear," said Frank sympathetically, handing the monster a tea towel to dry his tears. "What can we do? Let me think."

Frank and the monster sat holding hands while Frank racked his brains. Suddenly he leapt up. "I've got it, I've got an idea."

"Oooh," cried the monster. "You gave me a fright there, my boy Frank. All right then, what's the idea?"

"When I went to the video shop to get *Frankenstein* out there was another video called *Brides of Frankenstein*. Come on, let's go down to the video shop."

Later that night Frank and the monster sat together in the monster's hut watching the film and eating pop corn. In the film, Frankenstein made a lady monster to be a mate for the other monster.

"That's it," cried Frank N. Stein. "We'll make you a lady monster. First thing tomorrow I'll call Mark and Achmed and Chris and Jason and we'll start building another monster."

.

"Girls might have a better idea about a lady monster," grumbled Steinasaurus Rex.

"You're right," said Frank. "As soon as I get to school tomorrow I'll see if the girls want to help."

"I can't wait," giggled the monster. "A lady monster and just for me."

The Lady Monster

The next day at school Frank told everyone in his class to be at a special meeting under the big oak tree in the playground.

At break the children all raced out and sat under the big tree, sipping their drinks and munching their snacks.

"What is it, Frank?" asked Achmed. "Has something happened to our monster?"

"Well, sort of," replied Frank. He told them all about Steinasaurus Rex being lonely and wanting a lady monster. He ended up saying, "so I had a brilliant idea, I told Steinasaurus Rex that we would build him a lady monster."

There was a stunned silence, broken only when Mark said, "But Frank, Steinasaurus Rex only came alive by chance."

"I know," agreed Frank. "But we could leave the lady monster outside until there's a thunderstorm and hope for the best."

"Sounds a bit dicey to me," grumbled Jason.

"I think you're all being really boring," announced Chris. "I can't wait to build another monster. I'm going to start tonight even if the rest of you won't."

"Good," said Frank, grinning. "And Steinasaurus was hoping that the girls would help. He thought you could make a really beautiful lady monster for him."

"Hands up which girls will help," shouted Achmed.

All the girl's hands shot up.

"Great!" cried Frank. "Steinasaurus Rex knew we could rely on you. Everyone start bringing their bits and pieces to my garden on Saturday morning, and we'll get going on the bride of Steinasaurus Rex."

Just then the bell rang and the children ran to get into line, calling out to Frank, "Don't worry, Frank, we'll build a super-duper lady monster. Tell Steinasaurus that his problems are over!"

On Saturday morning every member of Frank's class came up with something – an old fridge, tyres, boxes of every size and shape, old dresses, bits of lace, four hats, loads of old jewellery and much more besides.

"Put everything in the middle of the lawn," ordered Frank. "And then we can decide what we need."

Soon there was a huge pile of rubbish in the Stein's back garden. Mr Stein looked out of the window and groaned, "I don't believe it," he said and raced downstairs.

"What is going on Frank? What on earth is all this rubbish doing on my lawn?"

"We're going to build a lady monster for Steinasaurus Rex, Dad. My poor monster is sad and lonely and we want to help him."

"Oh no!" sighed Mr Stein. "Look, Frank, I'm very fond of dear old Steinasaurus Rex but I don't think we could cope with another monster around the place. There isn't room. This is a very average kind of house and garden, definitely not big enough for two monsters."

The children stood round Mr Stein looking miserable.

"But Dad," Frank said, "if Steinasaurus Rex had a wife he could go and live somewhere else. He wouldn't need us so much. He could live nearby and we could all still be friends but he'd be more independent."

"True," agreed Mr Stein. "Yes, you're quite right, Frank. All right kids, go on and make your monster. And good luck!"

So the children set to work building the monster. Steinasaurus Rex watched from his window and called encouragement and suggestions.

After a few hours the new monster began to look rather good. The girls collected some wood shavings and stuck them onto the saucepan that had been used as a head. It looked as though the monster had long blond ringlets. They then gave the monster eyes of blue beads with sequins all round them. The bright red mouth was made of red cloth and then the monster was given bright-pink cheeks.

"She looks so beautiful and healthy,"
sighed Steinasaurus Rex.

"We haven't finished yet," cried the children. "Just you wait and see how gorgeous we're going to make her."

All day the monster was worked on and improved. By the end of the day she lay on the lawn, wearing a long green skirt that Mrs Stein had run up, an orange top with brown sleeves that the children had pinned on her, four necklaces, earrings, a big straw hat from Marina Dodgson and a pair of red shoes made from painted shoe boxes.

"What do you think, Steinasaurus Rex?" asked the children eagerly.

"She's wonderful," said the monster, dreamily. "Just the kind of wife I want."

"Thank you everyone," cried Frank. "I think we've done a fantastic job. Mum says there's sausage rolls and a big cake for tea."

The children cheered.

"All we have to do," continued Frank, "is wait for a thunderstorm and the lightning that will bring my second monster to life."

Two weeks later the skies grew dark and overcast. It began to rain, and thunder. All the children rushed over the Frank's house and stood with their noses pressed against the French windows to see what would happen. Frank and Steinasaurus Rex sat in his hut, eagerly looking out of the window. It rained and rained, the lightning flashed through the sky and a tree nearby was hit and crashed to the ground. But the lady monster just got wetter and wetter, never showing even a flicker of life.

As the sun came out, the children filed into the garden and stood by the sodden monster, tears running down their faces.

Steinasaurus Rex banged his fists on the ground and wailed. "It didn't work, your silly old brilliant plan didn't work. My beautiful wife looks horrible. It's all your fault, Frank."

"Don't give up Steinasaurus Rex," said Frank. "We'll just have to find another way of bringing her to life."

"We'll patch her up," cried the children. "You'll see, we'll make her as good as new in two days."

"We'll put her in the garage so she won't get wet again." added Achmed.

"Yes," agreed the others, "and we'll make her even better than new. Just you wait and see, Steinasaurus Rex."

A Broken Heart

After the storm, Steinasaurus Rex shut himself in his hut and wouldn't talk to anyone, not even Frank. The children worked hard to get the lady monster back to her former glory. In two days she was propped against the back wall of the garage, looking better than she had before.

"Come on, Steinasaurus Rex," said Frank, holding out his hand. "Come and see your lady friend. She's looking great!"

The monster let himself to be led to the garage, where all the children were waiting expectantly. Jason and Lucy flung open the doors of the garage, grinning broadly.

Steinasaurus Rex looked at the lifeless monster and shook his head and said, "I'm very sad, my boy Frank, very sad indeed."

He walked back to his hut, hunching his shoulders and shaking his head.

41

As the days passed the monster stopped eating. Everyone was very worried. The dustmen came round with a whole dustbin full of banana skins.

"They're his favourite," they told the Steins. "Just put them outside his door and he won't be able to resist the smell."

But the next morning the banana skins were still there.

After a while tips began to fill up again, and no one knew what to do.

"Why don't we phone Marina Dodgson?" suggested Mrs Stein. "Our monster liked her, maybe she can help."

The next day the film star turned up with a bunch of roses. Steinasaurus Rex livened up a bit when he saw her and ate the roses.

"Everyone is so worried about you, Steinasaurus, what can we do to make you feel better?"

"Bring my beautiful lady to life," begged the monster.

"Well, maybe next time there's a really

good thunderstorm the lightning will strike and wake her up."

"No," groaned the monster, shaking his big head. "It won't happen. I love her so much but she'll never come alive, never, never!"

"Don't be so sure about that," said Marina Dodgson. "I've just had an idea."

"What idea?" asked the monster eagerly. "Go on, tell me. I really want to know."

"I've got to talk to Frank and his parents first and some other people. Then I'll let you know what I'm planning."

After that the monster cheered up enough to eat seventy-five rotten banana skins.

Marina Dodgson went to speak with the Steins.

"He doesn't believe that the lady monster will ever come to life. He says that he loves her very much and that's why he can't eat."

"He may be right about her never coming to life," said Mr Stein gloomily. "After all it was a freak that Steinasaurus was hit by lightning, we can't really expect it to happen again."

"I agree," sighed Mrs Stein. "The chances of it happening twice must be a million to one."

"I feel so guilty," groaned Frank. "I should never have got his hopes up."

"It's not your fault, Frank," said Marina Dodgson soothingly.

"It is, it is! I should never have let the boys at school persuade me to make a monster, even though my name is Frank N. Stein. I should have said no! Now poor old Steinasaurus Rex is alive and he is very unhappy and I can't help him."

"I think you are all giving up too easily," declared Marina Dodgson.

"Well if you've got a suggestion, we'd like to hear it," said Mr Stein.

"Well here it is," said the actress. "Why

did Dr Victor Frankenstein want to make a monster in the film."

"Because he was a scientist," cried Frank.

"Exactly! I think the time has come for us to ask the scientists for their help."

"Of course!" yelled Frank. "That's it. Marina you are a genius!" and he gave her a big hug. "Scientists may be able to give her an electric charge to bring her alive."

"It's all well and good saying 'Get scientists to help'," said Mr Stein. "But which scientists? And how do we contact them? And how do we pay them."

"That shouldn't be a problem," cried Mrs Stein. "I mean governments all over the world are worried because Steinasaurus isn't eating all the rubbish. They'll pay anything to get him back to work."

"Oh yes!" said Frank. "We can contact those government scientists who tested Steinasaurus when he first came to life. Now why didn't I think of that?"

"I think I've still got their number," said

Mr Stein, looking through his address book. "Yes, here is it, let's call them now, not a moment to lose."

The scientists were very keen to help.

"We read about it in the papers," said the chief scientist. "We're very sympathetic to poor old Steinasaurus. Of course we'll do whatever we can. It'll be a new challenge to all of us. We'll be around first thing tomorrow morning."

"Do you think they'll be able to do anything, Dad?" asked Frank.

"I don't know, Frank, but I certainly hope so. Because if they can't I don't know what we're going to do with your poor, sad monster!"

The Wonders of Science

On the dot of nine the government scientists arrived as promised. Frank was given some time off school so that he could explain to the scientists exactly what had happened.

"We made this monster out of bits and pieces, just like we made Steinasaurus Rex. But this time she won't come alive. Even the lightning didn't do it."

The scientists put on their white coats and walked round the monster, making notes and taking photographs, and asking exactly what had been used to make her.

"I think we should take her apart and find out exactly what materials are in there. Maybe we can add electrodes and some materials which will conduct electricity."

"Steinasaurus Rex mustn't see you do that," said Frank quickly. "He's upset enough as it is."

"Why don't you and I go and see him," suggested the chief scientist. "I got on with him extremely well when we last met. I'll try to make him see that all is well."

So Frank and the scientist went over to the monster's hut and found him lying on the floor staring at the ceiling. The scientist shook Steinasaurus by the hand and then told him they were going to do everything they could to bring his lady to life.

Steinasaurus nodded and said, "Thank you," in a tired voice.

"I brought you some sawdust and a few stethoscopes," said the chief scientist. "They were your particular favourites during your stay with us, if I remember rightly."

"Yes," agreed the monster. "I did like them once. Just leave them, please. I may try and eat a little later on."

"I could boil them up and make some sawdust and stethoscope soup," suggested Frank. "You like soup."

"No," sighed the monster. "Don't bother, my boy Frank."

"I've brought you some tapes, Steinasaurus – love songs. I thought you might like to listen to them."

The monster brightened up a little.

"Love songs, Frank. Are they sad ones? Where everyone gets a broken heart?"

"Oh yes," Frank told him. "They're all very sad. Shall I play them?"

Frank put on the tapes and, as they left, tears ran down the monster's big cheeks.

The scientist and Frank went back into the garage. The lady monster lay on the floor in dozens of pieces.

"Please be quick," said Frank, "This would really upset Steinasaurus."

The scientists worked in pairs noting quickly what the lady monster was made of and then putting the pieces back. Soon she was as good as new.

"We've put lots of wires and batteries and fuses in her," they told Frank. "Now we're going to put a big electrical charge through her."

Some of the scientists were on ladders attaching things to the monster's head, others were putting wires around her feet.

"The charge is about the same as a direct hit by lightning," the scientists told Frank. "Fingers crossed, here we go."

The chief scientist pressed three switches. The monster shook for a minute or two and then slumped back as before.

"It didn't work," said Frank sadly.

"There was always only a very small chance that it would," said the chief scientist sadly. "We'll give it another try but don't get your hopes up too much."

They tried once more with exactly the same result.

"What a good thing Steinasaurus Rex didn't know what was going on in here." commented the chief scientist.

At that moment there was a terrible roar and Steinasaurus Rex reached into the garage and grabbed two of the scientists. He held them in his huge hands and glared at them.

"What have you been doing to my girlfriend? Have you been hurting her?"

"No, honestly!" squeaked the terrified scientists. "We were trying to bring her to life for you."

"Steinasaurus," shouted Frank in a stern voice. "Put those two nice people down this very minute, they have only been trying to help. No one has hurt your lady monster I promise you."

Steinasaurus Rex looked at Frank and then at the scientists and then back to his lady love.

"Come on, Steinasaurus, put them down or I won't be your friend any more."

The monster put the scientists down very gently.

"Now apologise," insisted Frank. "We've all been working very hard to help you."

"Sorry my boy Frank. Sorry scientists," mumbled the monster, and he stumbled back to his hut.

"Oh dear, he is in a bad way, poor chap," said the chief scientist. "I just wish there was something the world of science could do to help."

"We'll all work on it back at the lab," they promised, "but the chances of a breakthrough are very small."

After that the monster stopped eating all together and rubbish began to be a problem again all over the world.

Then one day Marina Dodgson arrived and announced, "I've got an idea."

"Alright," sighed Frank. "Let's hear it."

"I think the first thing we should do is get the lady monster out of the garage and put her on the lawn outside Steinasaurus's hut."

"Last time she just got drenched."

"I know, but today it's lovely and sunny," Marina Dodgson pointed out, "not a cloud in the sky."

"OK, so we get her out and then what?" demanded Frank.

"Then all the people who love Steinasaurus Rex make circles round the garden and we close our eyes and hold hands and hope and hope, as hard as we can, that she comes to life."

"That's the daftest thing I ever heard," scoffed Frank.

"We could try it at least," snapped the actress. "It couldn't do any harm."

"I suppose not," muttered Frank. "But you go and tell everyone what you want them to do. I would feel like a real idiot asking people to, well, just hope."

But to Frank's surprise, everyone was very willing to help.

So at twelve o'clock on Saturday four huge circles were formed round the Stein's house. Everyone who knew Steinasaurus Rex was there. On radio and television all over the world the call had gone out for people to close their eyes at the same time and join the 'Hope-In'. In some countries people had to wake up in the middle of the night to take part.

"This is silly," grumbled Frank, as he went over to Steinasaurus's hut to explain what was going on.

"Monster, all over the world people are closing their eyes and hoping for your lady monster to come alive. There are about 2,000 people gathered outside here alone, just for that purpose."

"We're calling it a 'Hope-In'," Marina Dodgson explained. "We've asked everyone who likes you and everyone who cares about the environment to come and join in. Millions of people will be hoping that your story has a happy ending."

"When does it start, my boy Frank?"

"In one minute," Frank told him.

Steinasaurus grabbed one of Frank's hands and one of Marina Dodgson's and they all closed their eyes tight. Then they heard the church clock strike twelve. Then there was a long silence.

Suddenly a big booming voice rang out, "Steinasaurus Rex, after all the fuss you've been making where are you?"

Hardly daring to hope, they all opened their eyes. There, standing with her hands

on her hips, stood the lady monster.

"She's alive! We all hoped her to life. Oh thank you everyone," yelled Steinasaurus Rex. "My true love is alive," and he ran across the lawn and hugged the lady monster.

Everyone cheered and cheered.

Steinasaurus jumped up and down and then shouted, "I'm starving."

"Me too!" declared the lady monster.

Then before anyone could stop them, they started to eat the tiles off the house.

"Stop!" yelled Frank.

Of course neither monster took any notice. Within minutes the Stein's house was stripped bare. The crowd gathered for the 'Hope-In' watched in amazement as the monsters munched contentedly.

"Frank," said Mr Stein. "We are going to change your name by deed poll. We are going to drop the Norman and then I forbid you to build any more monsters."

"Don't worry, Dad," sighed Frank. "I don't want to. Two are more than enough and I'll be very glad not to be Frank N. Stein any more!